The Key

Written by Tom Ottway
Illustrated by Barry Ablett

Collins

Who's in this story?

Listen and say 

 Download the audio at www.collins.co.uk/839723

Grandma
Grandpa
Ella

2 Hi! I'm Ella. I'm 7 years old. This is my brother, Liam. He's 6. This is Grandma and Grandpa. We enjoy seeing them. They're great. And now they have a new house! We stayed with them for a week.

Their new house has lots of rooms.

On Saturday, we played in their garden all day. It was fun! Grandma and Grandpa often make new games for us!

Liam was very good at the game, but I was better!

On Sunday, we were sad.

“What’s the matter?” asked Grandma.

“We want to play in the garden,” I said.

“I love the garden,” said Liam.

“But look out of the window,” said Grandma. “We can’t go out.”

Grandpa had an idea. He put down his book.

"Ella, Liam, can you help me?" he said.

Grandpa showed us a key. It was very big and very old.

"I found this key," he said. "I don't know what it's for."

This was exciting!

“We can find what it’s for,” I said.

“Yes!” said Liam, “Let’s go, Ella!”

Liam and I went into the hall. It was very long.

"What needs a key?" I said to Liam.

We tried to open all the boxes and the clock with the key.

Then we saw a small door.
"Try this door!" I said.
"No, the key is too big!" said Liam.
"Let me try," I said.

And then the door opened!

Behind the door, there were some stairs. We walked up the stairs and found a big room at the top of the house. There were lots of things in the room.

We played on the horse. It was fun.
After that, we were very hot!

"Look," said Liam. "There's an old key in the horse's mouth!"

This key was smaller.

"What does it open?" I asked Liam.
Then I saw a small door behind the horse.
We put the key in the door. It opened!

"Look! There are some stairs!" said Liam.

We were in a big room. There was a big, green table with some balls on it. Our names were on the board.

“How do we play?” asked Liam.

“Do we use this white ball?” I said.

Under the ball … there was a small key!

“Look, there’s the door,” said Liam.

The next door opened! Now we were in a long, glass room with lots of flowers and plants.

Then Liam looked up.

"Look! A key on a tree!" he said.

I jumped up and got the key.
"Well done, Ella!" said Liam.

"Let's find the door," I said.

We opened the door … we were in the kitchen again with Grandma and Grandpa!

"You did it!" said Grandpa. "Well done!"

“Come and eat some cake,” said Grandma.

Our grandparents are the best grandparents!

Picture dictionary

Listen and repeat 

fun

glass

grandparents

hall

key

stairs

1 Look and order the story

2 Listen and say

Collins

Published by Collins
An imprint of HarperCollins*Publishers*
Westerhill Road
Bishopbriggs
Glasgow
G64 2QT

HarperCollins*Publishers*
1st Floor, Watermarque Building
Ringsend Road
Dublin 4
Ireland

William Collins' dream of knowledge for all began with the publication of his first book in 1819.

A self-educated mill worker, he not only enriched millions of lives, but also founded a flourishing publishing house. Today, staying true to this spirit, Collins books are packed with inspiration, innovation and practical expertise. They place you at the centre of a world of possibility and give you exactly what you need to explore it.

10 9 8 7 6 5 4 3 2

ISBN 978-0-00-839723-4

www.collins.co.uk/elt

British Library Cataloguing in Publication Data

A catalogue record for this publication is available from the British Library.

Author: Tom Ottway
Illustrator: Barry Ablett (Beehive)
Series editor: Rebecca Adlard
Commissioning editor: Zoë Clarke
Publishing manager: Lisa Todd
Product managers: Jennifer Hall and Caroline Green
In-house editor: Alma Puts Keren
Project manager: Emily Hooton
Editor: Barbara MacKay
Proofreaders: Natalie Murray and Michael Lamb
Cover designer: Kevin Robbins
Typesetter: 2Hoots Publishing Services Ltd
Audio produced by id audio, London
Reading guide author: Emma Wilkinson
Production controller: Rachel Weaver
Printed and bound by: GPS Group, Slovenia

MIX
Paper from responsible sources
FSC™ C007454

This book is produced from independently certified FSC™ paper to ensure responsible forest management.

For more information visit: **www.harpercollins.co.uk/green**

Download the audio for this book and a reading guide for parents and teachers at www.collins.co.uk/839723